Sweetest little one with eyes so bright,
in my heart, you bring delight.
As your Auntie, here's my vow,
to love you always, starting now.

I'll be your rock, your trusted friend,
from start to finish, until the end.
Whenever you need me, I'll be near,
to hug you tight and calm your fear.

You're cute and sweet, with a heart so true,
I'm honored to be a part of you.
Through highs and lows, I'll be by your side,
with loving arms, I'll be your guide.

Love,
Your Auntie

I'll be your shelter in the storm,
holding you tight and keeping you safe.

I'll be your cheerleader,
celebrating every milestone, big or small.

I'll wipe away your tears
with gentle kisses and warm hugs.

I'll teach you about the wonders of nature,
from flowers in bloom to stars in the sky.

I'll be your secret keeper,
listening to your dreams and fears
with an open heart.

I'll be your guide through life's twists and turns,
helping you find your way.

I'll be your biggest fan,
applauding your uniqueness and
cheering you on.

I'll share with you the magic of imagination,
where dreams take flight
and anything is possible.

I'll be your rock when the world feels shaky,
offering strength and reassurance.

I'll be your rainbow on rainy days,
bringing color and joy to your world.

I'll be your playmate in the sunshine,
dancing and laughing in the warmth of the day.

I'll be your bedtime storyteller,
weaving tales of magic and wonder
until you drift off to sleep.

I'll be your source of encouragement,
helping you believe in yourself
and your dreams.

I'll be your confidante,
listening and offering wisdom
beyond my years.

I'll be your guardian,
watching over you with love and care,
wherever you may roam.

I'll be your partner in adventure,
exploring new horizons and creating memories
that sparkle like stars.

I'll be your source of laughter,
sharing jokes and silly moments
that light up even the darkest days.

I'll be your mentor in kindness,
showing you the power of compassion
and the beauty of a generous heart.

I promise to be the best
Auntie I can be and keep a
special place for you in
my heart, always. XO

a little note for you

Made in United States
Cleveland, OH
24 December 2024